Horace P. Tuttle

MAGICIAN EXTRAORDINAIRE!

Christine M. Schneider

Walker & Company ✸ New York

For Dad and Brian
with special thanks to Estelle

First published in the United States of America in 2001 by
Walker Publishing Company, Inc.

Published simultaneously in Canada by Fitzhenry and Whiteside, Markham, Ontario
L3R 4T8

Library of Congress Cataloging-in-Publication Data

Schneider, Christine M.
Horace P. Tuttle, magician extraordinaire / Christine M. Schneider.
p. cm.
Summary: A magician and his assistants are not happy working together,
but find that things do not go well when they are apart.
ISBN 0-8027-8788-6 -- ISBN 0-8027-8789-4
[1. Magicians--Fiction. 2. Interpersonal relationships--Fiction. 3. Humorous
stories.] I. Title.

PZ7.S3623 Ho 2001
[E]--dc21   2001017875

Book design by Christine M. Schneider and Sophie Ye Chin
Printed in Hong Kong

2 4 6 8 10 9 7 5 3 1

Horace P. Tuttle, Magician Extraordinaire, held a gleaming sword high above his head. It flashed in the bright stage lights as he swung it through the air. The audience ooohed and aaahed as he plunged it into The Daringly Dangerous Sword Trick box. "OUCH!" squealed Trixie from inside. "SHHH!" whispered Horace as he tried to smile at the audience.

He planned to pull a rabbit out of an empty hat next. But as he showed the hat to the crowd, Irwin sneezed from his pocket. "AAAAA-CHOOOO!" Horace tried to ignore Irwin's sniffling as he pulled him out of the hat.

Next, he waved a silken scarf in front of the audience and POOF! a lovebird
appeared out of thin air. No one but Horace seemed to notice that the bird was moping.
The audience applauded as the curtain closed, but Horace was angry.

"You ruined my show!" Horace told Trixie and Irwin back in the dressing room.

"How is the audience supposed to believe my magic tricks if you keep shrieking and sneezing?"

"It would help if you didn't prick me with swords when I'm in the box!" Trixie complained.

Irwin sneezed again. "I can't help it if I'm allergic to lint!" the rabbit sniffled.

"Why were you pouting onstage, you crazy dove?" he asked Gordon angrily.

"I'm not a dove," whined Gordon. "I'm a lovebird. And I miss my sweetie!"

"You are such ungrateful employees!" Horace retorted. "It's *my* show—*my* name is up in lights! People come to see *me*. If you don't like it, you can leave. I can do the show on my own!"

"That's it! I quit!" Trixie stormed out of the dressing room.

"Sayonara! We're through!" Irwin hopped out the door.

"Bye-bye, buster. You're on your own!" Gordon flew after them.

"Fine!" Horace yelled. "I don't need any of you!" and he slammed the door.

The next day, Horace rehearsed by himself
for that night's performance. He tested The Daringly
Dangerous Sword Trick on a sack of potatoes.
During the show, he figured, he would use
a volunteer from the audience. Horace
inserted the swords with the usual
zeal and flourishes.

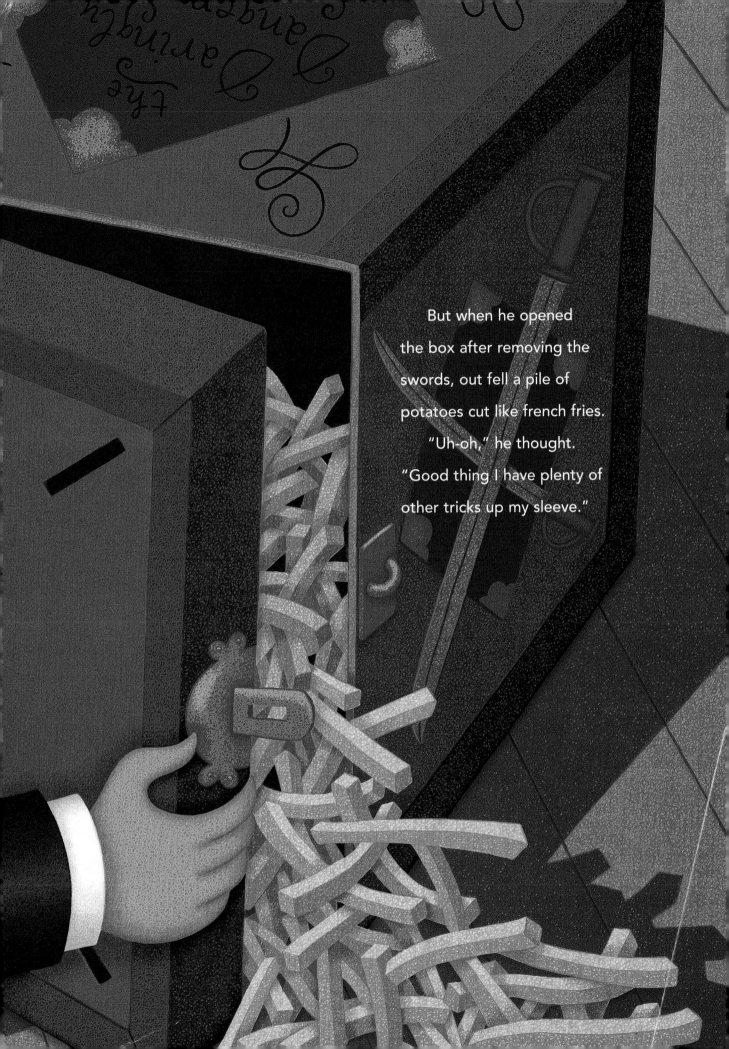

But when he opened
the box after removing the
swords, out fell a pile of
potatoes cut like french fries.
"Uh-oh," he thought.
"Good thing I have plenty of
other tricks up my sleeve."

Horace reached up his sleeve, but all he found was a tangled mess of scarves. "Rats!" he grumbled. "What can I hide up my sleeve that will surprise the audience?"

He searched around the room, but all he could find were wilted daisies and a very slippery goldfish.

So much for that trick.

Horace was getting desperate. He needed a foolproof trick to pull off the show tonight. The only one he had left was the old Pulling-the-Rabbit-Out-of-the-Hat Trick. And he had no rabbit. What else could he pull out of his hat?

A slimy bar of soap?

Some grimy galoshes?

A stinky piece of swiss?

Magic Made Easy

Things were not looking good. He paced around the dressing room. "Think, Horace!" he scolded himself. "There's got to be something!" And as he took one more look around the room, he knew exactly what—or whom—to pull out of his hat.

Just in time! As Horace grabbed his hat, he heard the announcer.

"Ladies and gentlemen, Horace P. Tuttle . . . Magician Extraordinaire!" The audience clapped and cheered as Horace raced into the spotlight.

"For my first illusion, I need a volunteer," Horace announced. He was nervous, but he took a deep breath and pulled a woman onto the stage.

"Choose a card, and I will guess what it is," he told her. She pulled a card out, and giggled.

"Queen of hearts!" Horace proclaimed.

"Nope!" she laughed.

This trick never failed! He tried again, "Ace of spades?"

"Wrong," she replied. "It's Jumpin' Jack Jensen, shortstop for the Pompano Pirates," she read, and the audience roared with laughter.

Somehow, his baseball cards had gotten mixed in with the trick cards!

"Never mind the silly card tricks!" Horace
tried to quiet the audience. "Behold! The Magic
Top Hat!" He held each arm out so that they
could see there was nothing up his sleeves. He
waved the hat in front of the crowd to show that
it was empty and tapped it with his wand. He
looked up at the audience mysteriously. The
room was silent with suspense.

Horace reached into the hat and groped around.
To his surprise, he found nothing. He smiled
nervously at the audience and peered into
the hat.

"Lenny!" He panicked. "Where are you?"
Horace shook the hat but still couldn't find Lenny.

He turned it upside down. Nothing.
He looked up his sleeves. Still nothing.

But just as he checked his pockets, he heard a scream from the audience. Then another. Soon the whole front row was shrieking and jumping up and down in their seats. Now Horace knew exactly where Lenny, his pet lizard, was.

"What a disaster!" Horace moaned. "Tomorrow night," he told himself, "it will be better."

But he was wrong. The next night, he couldn't get The Mystical Magical Rings apart at all. And when he tried to escape from The Wretched Rope Trick, he couldn't even budge. Two men from the audience finally had to climb onto the stage and untie him.

Fabulous Fleas!

7 o'clock nightly

It only got worse as the weeks went on. His reputation went down the drain. People in the audience chanted, "Horace, don't bore us!" Worst of all, he was replaced at the theater by another act.

Horace was reduced to performing magic on the street corner. A crowd gathered as he tried to levitate a lobster. But instead of rising off the table, the lobster pinched his nose and wouldn't let go.

Horace yelped, but everyone just laughed. Then someone pushed their way through the crowd. "Here, let me help you," said a kind voice. His nose throbbing, Horace looked up. He was surprised to see three familiar faces.

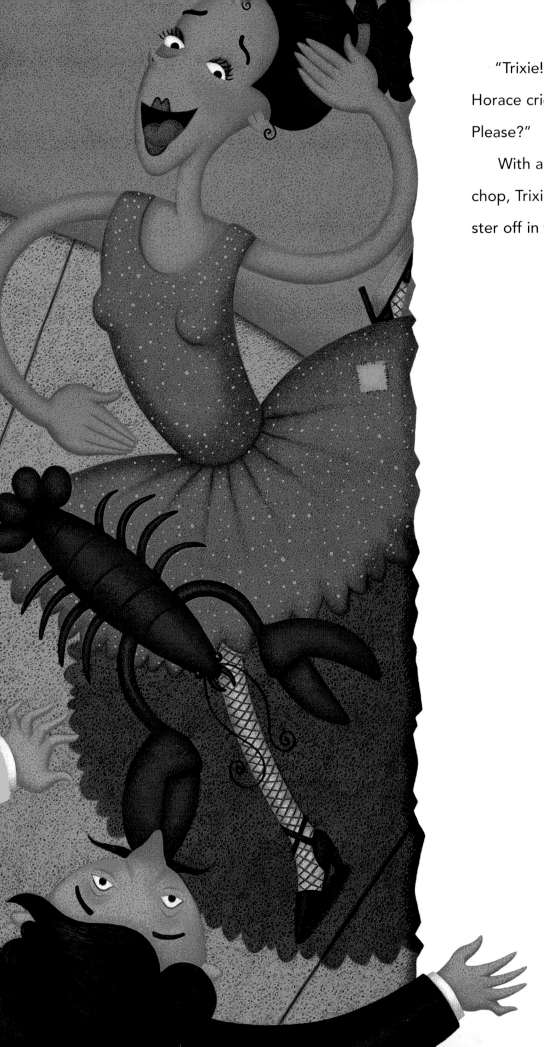

"Trixie! Irwin! Gordon!"
Horace cried. "Help me!
Please?"

With a swift karate
chop, Trixie had the lob-
ster off in two seconds flat.

"Oh, Trixie! I can't thank you enough!" Horace said as she put a bandage on his nose.

"It seems as if your show isn't doing very well," Irwin commented.

"No," Horace admitted. "Ever since the three of you left, it's been a disaster."

"Things haven't gone very well for us, either," said Gordon.

"I don't suppose you'd be willing to try it again as a team?" Horace asked.

"Perhaps," said Trixie. "But some things would have to change. You definitely need more practice with that sword trick. And I need a new costume."

"I'd like clean pockets, and more carrots for lunch," said Irwin.

"Could Clara, my love-muffin, join the show?" asked Gordon.

"That all sounds more than fair," replied Horace.

"Then it's a deal!" finished Trixie.

See the Marvelous Magic of The 5 Fantasticoes!

Friday night, the five of them stood in the wings, new costumes and lint-free pockets for all. The announcer stepped into the spotlight to introduce the show, and Horace glanced at his friends. "I can already tell," he whispered as the curtain rose, "this will be our most dazzling show ever!"